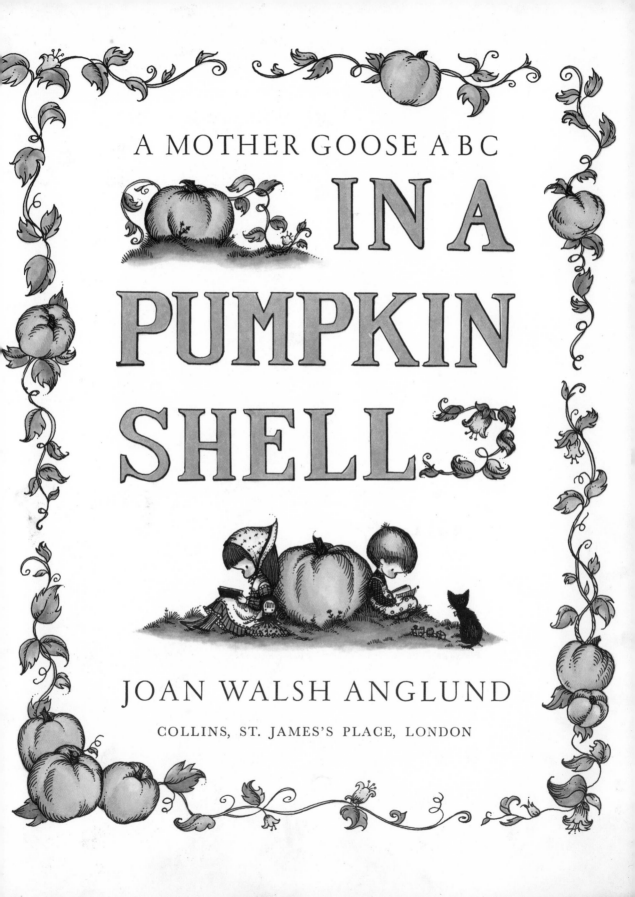

A MOTHER GOOSE A B C
IN A
PUMPKIN
SHELL

JOAN WALSH ANGLUND

COLLINS, ST. JAMES'S PLACE, LONDON

Other Books by
Joan Walsh Anglund

A FRIEND IS SOMEONE WHO LIKES YOU
LOVE IS A SPECIAL WAY OF FEELING
IN A PUMPKIN SHELL
CHRISTMAS IS A TIME OF GIVING
SPRING IS A NEW BEGINNING
CHILDHOOD IS A TIME OF INNOCENCE
WHAT COLOUR IS LOVE?
NIBBLE NIBBLE MOUSEKIN
THE COWBOY'S CHRISTMAS
A CHILD'S BOOK OF OLD NURSERY RHYMES
MORNING IS A LITTLE CHILD
DO YOU LOVE SOMEONE?

ISBN 0 00 193201 2

© 1960 BY JOAN WALSH ANGLUND
FIRST PUBLISHED IN GREAT BRITAIN 1961
PRINTED IN GREAT BRITAIN
COLLINS CLEAR-TYPE PRESS: LONDON AND GLASGOW

for all my little pumpkins...

colleen
brett
chel
karen
pam
larry
madeleine

APPLE

If I were an apple
And grew on a tree,
I think I'd drop down
On a nice boy like me.

I wouldn't stay there
Giving nobody joy;
I'd fall down at once
And say, "Eat me, my boy!"

B

BED

Little folks, little folks,
Now then for bed!
A pillow is waiting
For each little head.

Sleep all the night,
And wake in the morn;
Robert shall sound
The call on his horn.

C

CLOCK

Hickory, dickory, dock!
The mouse ran up the clock;
The clock struck one,
And down he run,
Hickory, dickory, dock.

DOG

Old Mother Hubbard
Went to the cupboard
To get her poor dog a bone;
When she got there,
The cupboard was bare,
And so the poor dog had none.

E EARLY

Early to bed, early to rise,
Makes a man healthy,
Wealthy and wise.

F FISH

Little Tommy Tittlemouse
Lived in a little house.
He caught fishes
In other men's ditches.

G GIRL

There was a little girl, and she had a little curl
Right in the middle of her forehead;
When she was good, she was very, very good,
But when she was bad, she was horrid.

H HEN

Hickety pickety, my black hen,
She lays eggs for gentlemen;
Gentlemen come every day
To see what my black hen doth lay.

I INK

If all the world were apple pie,
And all the sea were ink,
And all the trees were bread and cheese,
What should we have to drink?

J JUMP

Jack, be nimble,
Jack, be quick,
Jack, jump over the candlestick.

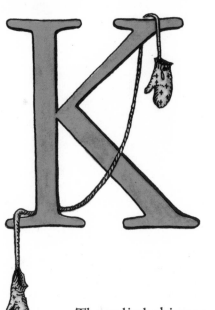

K

KITTEN

Three little kittens, they lost their mittens,
And they began to cry,
"Oh, Mother, dear, we greatly fear,
That we have lost our mittens."

"What! lost your mittens, you naughty kittens!
   Then you shall have no pie."
   Mee-ow, mee-ow, mee-ow, mee-ow,
   Then you shall have no pie.

L LOVE

I love you well, my little brother,
And you are fond of me;
Let us be kind to one another,
As brothers ought to be.
You shall learn to play with me,
And learn to use my toys;
And then I think that we shall be
Two happy little boys.

M MICE

Three blind mice, see how they run!
They all ran after the farmer's wife,
Who cut off their tails with the carving knife,
Did you ever see such a sight in your life
As three blind mice?

N

NUT

I had a little nut tree; nothing would it bear
But a silver nutmeg and a golden pear.
The King of Spain's daughter came to visit me,
And all for the sake of my little nut tree.
I skipped over water, I danced over sea,
And all the birds in the air couldn't catch me.

O OWL

Bow-wow says the dog;
Mew, mew, says the cat;
Grunt, grunt, goes the hog;
And squeak says the rat.

Tu-whu says the owl;
Caw, caw, says the crow;
Quack, quack, goes the duck;
And moo says the cow.

P

PUMPKIN

Peter, Peter, pumpkin eater,
Had a wife and couldn't keep her;
He put her in a pumpkin shell,
And there he kept her very well.

Q

QUEEN

The Queen of Hearts,
She made some tarts,
All on a summer's day.
The Knave of Hearts,
He stole the tarts,
And took them clean away.

The King of Hearts
Called for the tarts,
And beat the knave full sore.
The Knave of Hearts
Brought back the tarts,
And vowed he'd steal no more.

R RAIN

Rain, rain, go away,
Come again another day;
Little Johnny wants to play.

S SHOE

There was an old woman who lived in a shoe.
She had so many children she didn't know what to do.
She gave them some broth, without any bread.
She whipped them all soundly and sent them to bed.

T THANK

Thank You for the earth so sweet,
Thank You for the things we eat,
Thank You for the birds that sing,
Thank You, God, for everything.

U

UNICORN

The lion and the unicorn
Were fighting for the crown;
The lion beat the unicorn
All round the town.
Some gave them white bread,
And some gave them brown;
Some gave them plum cake,
And sent them out of town.

V

VELVET

Hark! Hark! The dogs do bark!
The beggars are coming to town;
Some in rags and some in tags,
And some in velvet gowns.

W WATER

Little drops of water,
Little grains of sand,
Make the mighty ocean,
And the pleasant land.